DO NOT REMOVE CARD

GUS and GRANDPA
at the Hospital

Claudia Mills ★ Pictures by Catherine Stock

Farrar, Straus and Giroux

New York

To my mother,
grand-mère extraordinaire
—C.M.

For Felix, Sheila, and everyone at
Terence Cardinal Cooke Health Care Center
—C.S.

Text copyright © 1998 by Claudia Mills
Illustrations copyright © 1998 by Catherine Stock
All rights reserved
Distributed in Canada by Douglas & McIntyre Ltd.
Color separations by Berryville Graphics / All Systems Color
Printed in the United States of America
Designed by Filomena Tuosto
First edition, 1998

Library of Congress Cataloging-in-Publication Data
Mills, Claudia.
Gus and Grandpa at the hospital / Claudia Mills ; pictures
by Catherine Stock. — 1st ed.
p.   cm.
Summary: Gus must visit the hospital when his beloved
Grandpa has a heart attack.
ISBN 0-374-32827-7
[1. Grandfathers—Fiction. 2. Hospitals—Fiction.]
I. Stock, Catherine, ill. II. Title.
PZ7.M63963Gue   1998
[E]—dc21   97-20609

Contents

Mr. Skipper Q. Dog

Gus and Grandpa
loved to get mail.
Gus's mother didn't.
"It's all bills," she said.

Gus's father didn't, either.
"It's all junk," he said.

But all summer long
Gus and Grandpa
looked out the window
every day at lunchtime
to see if the mail truck
had come yet.

At Gus's house,
the mail came
through a boring mail slot
in the boring front door.
At Grandpa's house,
the mail came
in a real mailbox
by the side of the road
across from the railroad tracks.
Grandpa had made the mailbox.
It was a little wooden house
with a pointy roof,
two square windows,
and a bright red door.

One day Gus and Grandpa
were waiting for the mail.
When the mail truck came,
Grandpa's dog, Skipper,
barked and barked.

"I'm a little tired today,"
said Grandpa.
"Will you get the mail for me?"
So Gus ran out to the box
by himself.
He carried the mail
in to Grandpa.

"What did we get?"
Grandpa asked.
There was a catalogue
from a biscuit company.
Gus and Grandpa
ordered some biscuit mix.
"Biscuits and gravy!"
Grandpa said.
"I can taste them already."

There was a letter
telling them how to
enter the lottery
and win ten million dollars.
Gus and Grandpa entered it.

There was one other letter.
It was from a dog food company.
"Look!" Gus said.
"It's for Skipper!"
Gus couldn't believe it.
He read the envelope again.
The letter was addressed to
Mr. Skipper Q. Dog.

"Once, I sent away
for some special dog food
for Skipper," Grandpa said.
"I guess all the
dog food companies
have his name now."

Gus showed Skipper his letter.
Skipper smelled it.
He walked away.

"Maybe Skipper
needs a mailbox,"
Grandpa said.
He and Gus made one
from an old oil can.
On the side, Grandpa painted
"Mr. Skipper Q. Dog."
Skipper didn't even look
at his mailbox.
Gus and Grandpa
put a bone in it.
Skipper looked at it then!

Grandpa said his chest hurt
from working so hard.
"I must be getting old,"
he said.

Grandpa lay on the couch.
Gus thought he must be
dreaming of biscuits and gravy.
Skipper lay beside his mailbox.
He was probably
dreaming of bones.
And Gus lay on the floor,
dreaming of ten million dollars.

The Hospital

When Gus woke up
the next morning,
Daddy was gone
and Mommy looked worried.
"Grandpa is very sick,"
she said.
"He had a heart attack.
He called us
in the middle of the night,
and Daddy took him
to the hospital."

Gus knew that
a heart attack was
something very bad.
He didn't want anything
even a little bit bad
to happen to Grandpa.
"I'm sure Grandpa
will be all right," Mommy said.
But she didn't sound sure.
"We can visit him
at the hospital tomorrow."

Gus and Mommy waited
all day by the phone.
Finally, Daddy called
with good news about Grandpa.
It would take time,
but Grandpa's heart
was going to get better.

The mail came.

Gus's parents got their own
entry form for the lottery.
Mommy helped Gus send it in.
Now he and Grandpa
had two chances to win.
Gus hoped they would win soon.
Ten million dollars
would help Grandpa to cheer up
in the hospital.

The next day,
Mommy took Gus
to the hospital to see Grandpa.
She led the way
down a long, long hall.
They passed room
after room after room.

The rooms had beds in them,
and people were lying in the beds.
The people wore green nightgowns.
They all looked sick.
Gus walked more slowly.
He didn't want to see Grandpa
lying in one of those beds,
wearing one of those nightgowns.

Mommy stopped
outside a door.
"This is Grandpa's room,"
she said.
"Grandpa may look strange.
He has a tube in his arm
and in his nose.
The tubes will help
Grandpa to get well."

Mommy went in.
Gus stayed in the hall.
He didn't want to see Grandpa
with helpful tubes in him.

21

Daddy came out.
He gave Gus a big hug.
He held Gus's hand.
Together they walked
into Grandpa's room.

Grandpa lay in the bed.
He was wearing a green nightgown.
There was a tube in his arm
and another tube in his nose.
Gus wanted to go home.

Grandpa smiled at Gus.
"My bed is too flat,"
he told Gus.
"Can you make the head
go up for me?"
He showed Gus

how to push the button.

Gus pushed the button.

"That's much better,"

Grandpa said.

Sitting up in bed,

Grandpa looked more like himself.

"Did you get any mail?"
Grandpa asked Gus.
Gus told him
about the second chance
to win ten million dollars.
"Cross your fingers,"
Grandpa said.

"Right." Gus smiled.

Then it was time to go.
Gus pushed the button
on Grandpa's bed
to help Grandpa
lie down again.
Grandpa closed his eyes,
and Mommy and Daddy and Gus
tiptoed away.

Waiting

Grandpa would be in the hospital
for a whole week.
Every day after work,
Daddy drove Mommy and Gus
to Grandpa's house.
Mommy checked Grandpa's
telephone messages.
Daddy watered Grandpa's plants
and turned on the sprinkler
in Grandpa's garden.

Gus took Grandpa's mail
out of the mailbox.
No biscuit mix.
No ten million dollars.
But Skipper got
two credit cards
and a catalogue
from a cheese company.
Gus put Skipper's mail
in Skipper's mailbox.
He put dog food
in Skipper's dog food bowl.
He put water
in Skipper's water bowl.

Gus helped Skipper
chase squirrels and magpies.
Gus hugged Skipper
and patted his fur.
Gus told Skipper,
"Grandpa is coming home
pretty soon."

From Grandpa's house,
Daddy drove Mommy and Gus
to the hospital.
By the middle of the week,
Grandpa was sitting up in bed
all the time
with no tubes anywhere.

By the end of the week,
Grandpa was sitting in a chair.

Gus knew all about hospitals now.
He knew how to find
Grandpa's room.
He knew how to find
the hospital soda machine.
Mommy and Daddy never gave him
quarters for the machine.
They said the soda
in the machine
was too expensive.
But Grandpa always gave
Gus three quarters.
"I think it's time
for some ginger ale,"
he would say.

Gus knew how to raise
the head and the foot
of Grandpa's bed.
He knew how to use
the remote control
on Grandpa's TV.

Gus knew the names
of the nurses
who came to Grandpa's room:
Susan, Marie, and Jack.
They gave him
paper and crayons
to make pictures for Grandpa.

All of that was fun.
Still, Gus wanted Grandpa
to come home.
He knew that Grandpa
felt the same way.
Grandpa sat in the chair
next to his one small window
and looked out
toward the mountains,
toward the railroad tracks,
toward the mailbox,
toward Skipper,
toward home.

Home Again

"Grandpa is coming home today!"
Mommy and Daddy told Gus.

"Grandpa is coming home today!"
Gus told Skipper.

Gus made a sign
for Grandpa's mailbox:
WELCOME HOME, GRANDPA!
Gus had a surprise
for Grandpa, too.
The biscuit mix had come!

Mommy and Daddy took Gus
to the hospital
for the last time.
On the ride home,
Grandpa looked out the window
as if he had never seen
a tree or a house
or a mountain before.

At home,
Skipper came running
to the gate.
Grandpa's eyes were wet
when he bent down stiffly
to pat Skipper.
"You took good care
of Skipper,"
he told Gus.
Gus felt proud.

Inside,
everyone talked and barked
all at once.
"Did today's mail come yet?"
Grandpa asked Gus.

Gus checked.
The box was full.

There were two get-well cards.
There was one catalogue
with shiny pictures of tents
and packs and camping stoves.
There was a letter asking Skipper
to join a book club.

"Where's our ten million dollars?"
Grandpa asked Gus.

"It didn't come today,"
Gus said.

"You know what, Gus?"
Grandpa said.
"I have a feeling that
it is never going to come.
I have a feeling that you and I
are not going to win the lottery."

Mommy was baking
a batch of biscuits
from the new biscuit mix.
Grandpa's house smelled
of golden, flaky biscuits
rising slowly in the oven.
Gus and Grandpa sniffed deeply.
Skipper's nose quivered.

Grandpa said,
"But you know what I think?
Being home
with you and Skipper
and your mom and dad
and biscuits and gravy
is better than ten million dollars."

Gus thought so, too.